For
James, Maria, and Gabriel

First published in Great Britain in 2000 by Orchard Books

First U.S. Edition

Simmons, Jane.
    Little Fern's first winter / Jane Simmons.
        p. cm.
    Summary: Fern and her brother Bracken play hide-and-seek as the other animals prepare for the first snowstorm of winter.
    ISBN 0-316-79667-0
    [1. Rabbits—Fiction. 2. Animals—Fiction. 3. Hide-and-seek—Fiction. 4. Snow—Fiction. 5. Brothers and sisters—Fiction.] I. Title.

PZ7.S59182 Li 2001
[E]—dc21   00-035417

10 9 8 7 6 5 4 3 2 1

Printed in Singapore

Little Fern's
First Winter

by Jane Simmons

Little, Brown and Company
BOSTON NEW YORK LONDON

"The snow is coming!" said Mama Rabbit.
"What's snow?" said Fern.
"It's lovely, fluffy stuff when it settles, but very, very cold," said Mama. "Go play with Bracken while I change the hay."

Fern and Bracken hopped
and flipped and giggled
together.

"Let's play hide-and-seek,"
said Fern. "I'll hide first."

"And I'll count," said
Bracken.

"1, 2, 3, 4 . . ."

Fern looked for somewhere to hide.
All the birds were swooping and chattering.
"The snow is coming! We must fly away!"
they squawked.

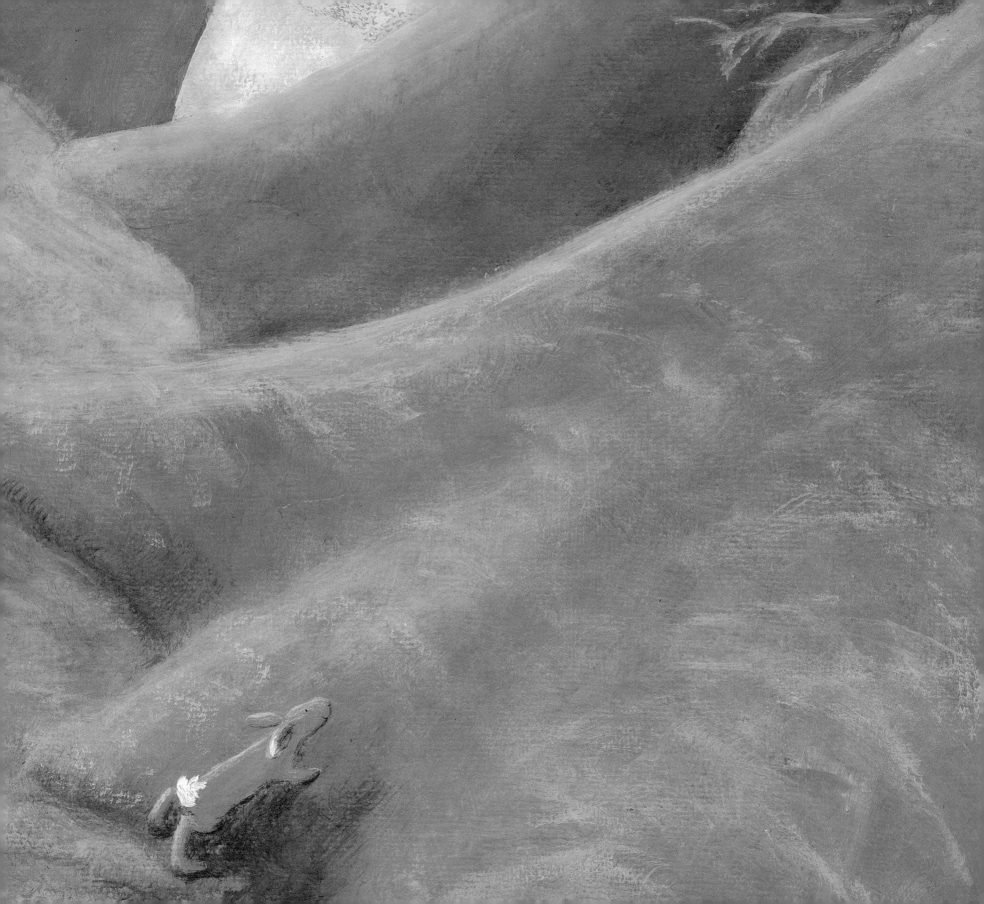

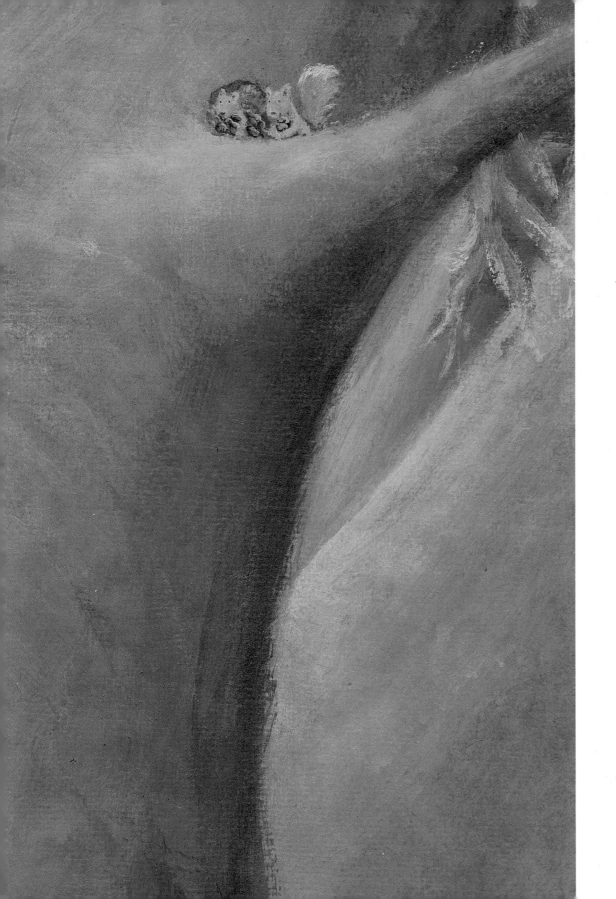

"Can I hide in your tree?" asked Fern.

"No! The snow is coming! We need the tree for our nuts," said Squirrel.

So Fern hopped on.

"Can I hide in your nest?" Fern asked the mice.

"The snow is coming! We need to sleep in our nest to stay warm," they said.

"Can I hide with you?" she asked the beetles, but they just crept away.

Fern couldn't find anywhere to hide.

"Found you!" shouted Bracken. And they hopped and flipped and giggled together.
"Now it's your turn to hide," said Fern, and she started to count.

"1, 2, 3, 4, 5, 6, 7, 8 . . ."

"... 9, 10! I'm coming!"

she shouted.
Everything was quiet in the woods.

There were no birds in
the sky . . .

no squirrels in the trees . . .

no mice in the grass . . .

no beetles under the leaves . . .

and no Bracken anywhere!

Fern went down the burrow under the ground.

"Mama, have you seen Bracken?" asked Fern.

"No, dear," said Mama Rabbit. "I've been changing the hay."

So Fern went up the burrow and outside again.

"Bracken, where are you?" said Fern. A chill wind whistled through the silent woods. Fern shivered.

"Bracken!" she called. Something cold and soft melted on her nose.

"Bracken!"

The whole woods had changed.
Was this snow?
"Where are you, Bracken?"
shouted Fern again.

BRACKEN!

"Fern," came a faint cry from deep in the snow. It sounded like Bracken! Fern dug and dug and dug . . .

and there at last was
Bracken.

"What's happening?" he
said, trembling.

"I think the snow has
come," said Fern. "Mama says
it's lovely when it settles."

So they huddled up as
close as close could be until
it stopped snowing.

Then they hopped and flipped
and giggled in the fluffy, cold snow.
"Fern! Bracken!" called Mama Rabbit.
"Time to come in."

And that night they all curled up
as close as close could be in the
warm, soft hay.